The honey bee is one of the smallest creatures in the world
but it may be the most important for life on Earth. It is the planet's
greatest pollinator — moving pollen from one plant to another,
causing flowers to produce seeds and fruits.

Honey bees can live in the wild or in boxes made by beekeepers.
A honey bee can't live alone. It's part of a family that works closely
together. A bee is always changing jobs: first she is a cleaner,
then a babysitter, a builder, a guard, a scout and finally a harvester.

This is the story of a scout...

For my first grandchild, Spencer Bond. R.H

To Dad — a farmer who understands bees. BL

First published 2013
by Walker Books Ltd
87 Vauxhall Walk
London SW11 5HJ

This edition published 2015

10 9 8 7 6 5 4 3 2 1

This book has been typeset in Din Schrift and Gill Sans Bold italic

Printed in China

British Library of Cataloguing in Publication Data: a catalogue
record for this book is available from the British Library

978-1-4063-5521-5

www.walker.co.uk

WALKER BOOKS
AND SUBSIDIARIES
LONDON · BOSTON · SYDNEY · AUCKLAND

Flight of the Honey Bee

RAYMOND HUBER

illustrated by BRIAN LOVELOCK

A bee the size of a cherry pip crawls from the hive. Her stripes glow golden in the morning sun. Scout has spent her whole life in the crowded hive. Now it is time to fly out and explore the world – time to search for flowers to collect pollen and nectar for food.

Her sister bees are inside making honey, but will there be enough? The cold is coming and Scout must find the last flowers of autumn.

There are 50,000 female bees in a hive, and very few males.

Scout's wings hum into life,
so fast they are almost invisible,
lifting her into the wide sky. She rises
in a spiral, up and away from the hive.

Scout remembers what she passes as
she flies, so later she can return home..
She knows the sun will guide her too.

*Bees navigate using sunlight, landmarks
and smell. They also have a magnetic
sense that is like a built-in compass.*

Scout flies swift and straight as an arrow.
The wind buffets her, ruffling the fine hairs
on her face. But she keeps on steadily and
rides out the rapids. Eyes as black as polished stones
are searching — seeking a splash of colour below.

An arresting smell drifts
on the breeze. Scout locks onto this scent.
She flies over a clearing, and spread before her
is a marvellous meadow — an ocean of flowers.

Bees are furry,
even their eyeballs.
The hairs help them sense
changes in the wind.

Bees have a powerful sense of smell.
They use their antennae to pick up scents.
Bees can smell in "stereo", each
antenna smelling a different direction.

11

A flash of feathers!

A hungry blackbird swoops for the kill.
But Scout zips down and escapes into the trees,
weaving between tangled twigs.

Many creatures eat honey bees,
including other insects like
wasps and dragonflies,
as well as spiders, frogs,
birds and mammals such
as bears and badgers.

When the coast is clear, Scout is drawn to the sea of flowers again.
She settles on a velvety petal and plunges her head into the flower.
Here is sunken treasure: a cup of sweet nectar. The tip of her tongue,
shaped like a miniature spoon, sips the syrup.

Scout zigs and zags from flower to flower, spreading pollen around.
The pollen clings to her fuzzy body — a sprinkle of sun-powder.

Bees are charged with static electricity during flight,
which attracts pollen to their bodies.
They have an extra stomach to carry nectar home.

Scout has finished drinking.
She must tell her sister bees about
this field of blue. But a thundercloud
cloaks the sun. All at once, the cloud bursts.
Rain batters Scout to the ground.
She crawls under a leaf as hailstone
bombs explode around her.

Bees avoid rain and storms.
Raindrops can damage them
and chill their wing muscles,
leaving them grounded.

16

Wasps invade beehives to steal honey and eat baby bees.

The downpour passes. Scout picks up
the scent of her hive and follows it.

Outside the hive there's a squad of guard bees.
A yellow-jacketed enemy is attacking. Scout knows
that twitchy way of flying — it's a wasp!

The wasp grabs Scout as she glides in to land.
It raises its sting but the guards move in,
wrestling the wasp with their legs.

Honey bees only sting
to defend themselves.
They will die after stinging
larger animals.

19

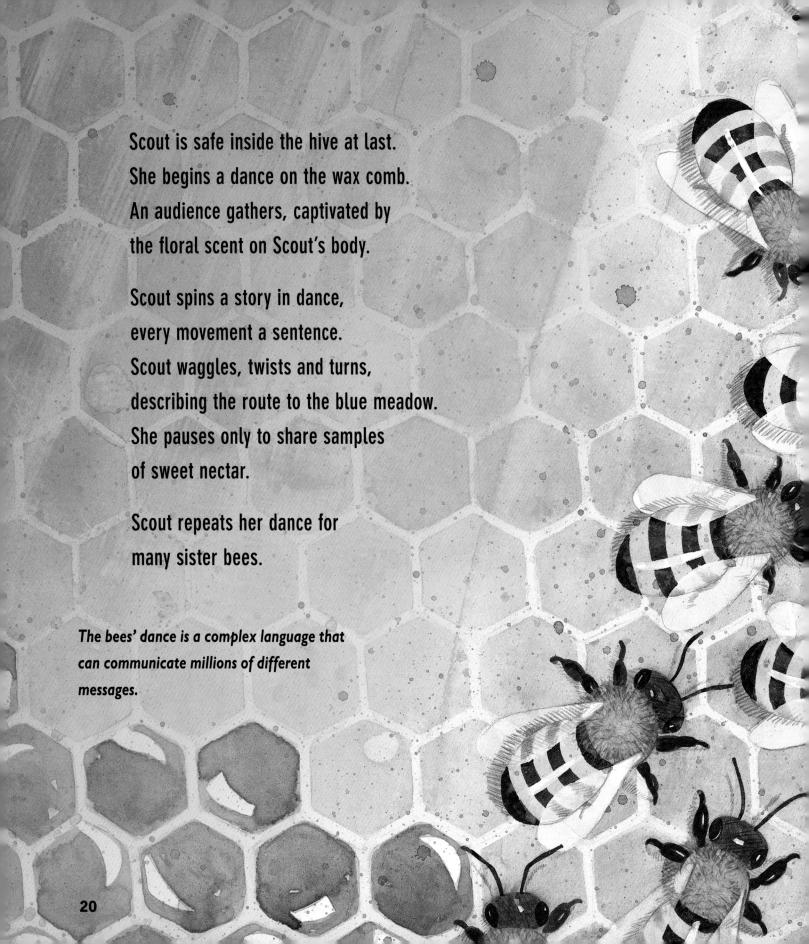

Scout is safe inside the hive at last.
She begins a dance on the wax comb.
An audience gathers, captivated by
the floral scent on Scout's body.

Scout spins a story in dance,
every movement a sentence.
Scout waggles, twists and turns,
describing the route to the blue meadow.
She pauses only to share samples
of sweet nectar.

Scout repeats her dance for
many sister bees.

The bees' dance is a complex language that
can communicate millions of different
messages.

Now that the sister bees know where
to find the meadow, hundreds of bees take off.
They flick from the hive like golden pebbles.

*Bees need to harvest nectar from
more than two million flowers
to make enough honey
to fill just one jar.*

Back in the hive, Scout passes her precious nectar
to the house bees. They put it in the comb
and fan it with their wings. The nectar will be
transformed into liquid gold — honey
for the bees to eat!

*Nectar is mostly water, until the bees
dry and thicken it by beating their wings,
converting it to honey.*

Scout visits the nursery where babysitter bees
pluck the pollen from her body and mix it
with honey to feed the babies.

*The queen can lay thousands of eggs a day. It is the job
of the few male bees in the hive to fertilize a new queen.*

Nearby sits the queen, long and lustrous.
She is mother of all the bees, laying eggs
that look like tiny grains of rice.

In its lifetime
a bee can travel
over 900 kilometres
on flower runs, until its
wings are worn out.

Exhausted after her mission, Scout rests her silvery wings for a spell.
Soon she will join her sister bees in the blue meadow for the autumn harvest.
With enough honey, her family can now survive the winter.

Scout's daring flight has been worth every beat of her wings.

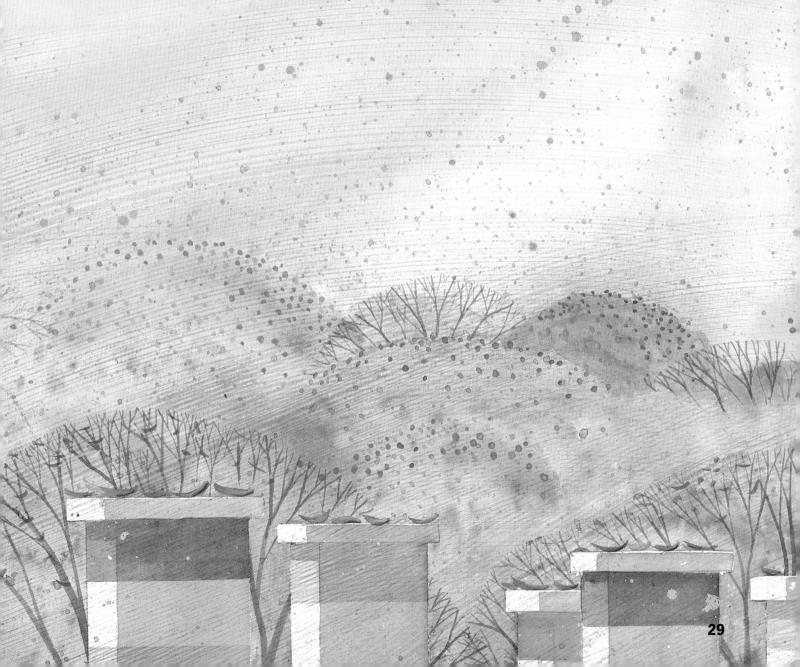

Save the bees!

Pollination by bees gives us delicious apples, cherries, strawberries, kiwifruit, nuts and many vegetables. But honey bees are in danger of dying out. You can help bees by giving them food and clean places to live.

Plant a variety of flowers, herbs and flowering trees.

Don't use toxic chemicals in gardens.

Don't pollute the air or water.

These steps will also help other pollinators, such as bumblebees, butterflies and other insects.

Look up the pages to find out about all these honey-bee things. Don't forget to look at both kinds of word – this kind and *this kind*.

Index

About the author

Raymond Huber has been a primary-school teacher, a gardener and a beekeeper, and is now an author and editor. He has a science degree, teaches science to all ages, and has written many science books for schools. He's also written two novels about a honey bee called Ziggy, of which *Sting* was a finalist in the New Zealand Post Book Awards. Raymond loves working in his garden and harvesting the fruit that bees have pollinated. His other hobbies include sculpting, cycling and writing about books and bees on his website www.raymondhuber.co.nz.

About the illustrator

Brian Lovelock is a scientist who has painted all his life but only recently started illustrating picture books. He likes strong composition, saturated colour and imaginative perspective, working mainly with watercolour, but also adding acrylic ink and coloured pencil. His first picture book, *Roadworks*, by Sally Sutton won the 2009 New Zealand Post Book Award for Best Picture Book. Brian has always loved picture books — the infinite variety of styles and the individuality that artists can impart to a book. His other interests include reading, cooking and spending time with his friends. He lives in Auckland, New Zealand.

Note to Parents

Sharing books with children is one of the best ways to help them learn. And it's one of the best ways they learn to read, too.

Nature Storybooks are beautifully illustrated, award-winning information picture books whose focus on animals has a strong appeal for children. They can be read as stories, revisited and enjoyed again and again, inviting children to become excited about a subject, to think and discover, and to want to find out more.

Each book is an adventure into the real world that broadens children's experience and develops their curiosity and understanding – and that's the best kind of learning there is.

Note to Teachers

Nature Storybooks provide memorable reading experiences for children in Key Stages 1 and 2 (Years 1–4), and also offer many learning opportunities for exploring a topic through words and pictures.

By working with the stories, either individually or together, children can respond to the animal world through a variety of activities, including drawing and painting, role play, talking and writing.

The books provide a rich starting-point for further research and for developing children's knowledge of information genres.

Nature Storybooks support the literacy curriculum in a variety of ways, providing:
- a focus for a whole class topic
- high-quality texts for guided reading
- a resource for the class read-aloud programme
- information texts for the class and school library for developing children's individual reading interests

Find more information on how to use Nature Storybooks in the classroom at
www.walker.co.uk/naturestorybooks
Nature Storybooks support KS 1–2 English and KS 1–2 Science